Other Kipper books:

KIPPER
KIPPER'S TOYBOX
KIPPER'S BIRTHDAY
KIPPER'S BOOK OF COUNTING
KIPPER'S BOOK OF COLOURS
KIPPER'S BOOK OF OPPOSITES
KIPPER'S BOOK OF WEATHER
WHERE, OH WHERE, IS KIPPER'S BEAR?
KIPPER'S SNOWY DAY
KIPPER'S CHRISTMAS EVE
KIPPER'S A TO Z
KIPPER AND ROLY
KIPPER'S MONSTER
KIPPER'S BALLOON

THE LITTLE KIPPER SERIES
THE LITTLE KIPPER COLLECTION
KIPPER STORY COLLECTION
THE 2ND LITTLE KIPPER COLLECTION

HB edition first published 2003
PB edition first published 2004
by Hodder Children's Books,
a division of Hodder Headline Limited,
338 Euston Road, London NW1 3BH
Copyright © Mick Inkpen 2003
10 9 8 7 6 5 4 3 2

ISBN 0 340 87901 7 PB

Kipper's Beach Ball

Mick Inkpen

Hodder
Children's
Books

A division of Hodder Headline Limited

One morning as Kipper was
pouring out his cornflakes,
a thing dropped into his bowl,
a colourful, wrinkly sort of thing.

Kipper picked up the thing and
looked at it. He sniffed it. It had a
nice, plasticky sort
of smell.

It was quite exciting
really, except that
Kipper had no idea
what the wrinkly,
plasticky thing
might be.

He hurried round to Tiger's house. 'I got a free gift in my cornflakes!' he said.

Tiger was unimpressed.

'Oh I've been collecting them for weeks,' he said. 'I've already got the penguin rubber that goes on the end of your pencil, the wind-up shark that goes in the bath, and TWO jumpy frogs. They're just for fun. The only one I haven't got yet is the ball. What's yours then?'

Kipper held up the thing.
'It must be the ball!' he said.
It didn't look much like a ball.
It didn't look much like anything.
'I thought balls were supposed
to be round and bouncy,' said Tiger.
Kipper bounced the thing.
Or rather he didn't, because the
thing just hit the floor with a little
'plap!' and no bounce at all.
It lay there looking colourful,
but useless.

It was then that they
discovered the nozzle.
'Oh!' said Tiger.
'You're meant to blow
it up! This isn't just an
ordinary ball! It's a Beach Ball!'
He started to blow it up.
He blew,
and blew,
and blew,
until he became giddy and
Kipper had to take over.
Slowly the wrinkly,
plasticky thing turned
into the fattest, shiniest,
beachiest ball they
had ever seen!

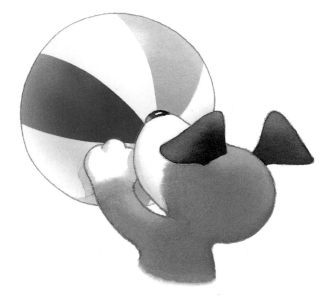

'WOW!' said Kipper.
He bounced the ball
as hard as he could.

'Wow!' said Tiger.

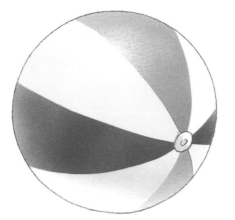

Where would you take a beach ball? To the beach, of course. And that is what they did.

Kipper was so excited as they reached the cliff top, he forgot how windy cliff tops are, and threw the ball up into the air. This was a mistake.

The wind grabbed the ball and whisked it away!

It sailed high out over the beach, circling in the air, making the seagulls squawk.

Then it dropped onto the hard sand and bounced up again, spinning faster and faster away from them.

'Stop!' called Kipper, chasing down the cliff steps. But the ball rushed away.

It looped and bounced and skidded along the beach, knocking the top off a sandcastle.

And just as it seemed that it would never, never stop...

The sea grabbed it. And for a moment it stopped spinning, as if to catch its breath, before a wave whooshed up the beach and sucked it out into the surf.

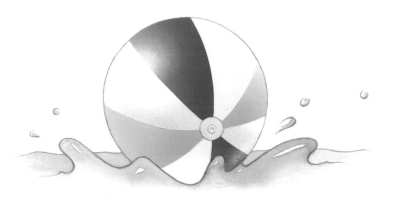

'Come back!' shouted Kipper. But by the time Kipper and Tiger reached the water's edge, the ball was bobbing far out among the waves.

'Come back!'

And strangely, the ball seemed
to do as it was told.

For at that moment a great
breaking wave came looming up
behind it, flicked it up onto its nose
like a seal, and began bringing it
back to the beach.

'It's coming! It's coming!'
screamed Tiger. 'Get ready Kipper!'

There was no time to get ready.
Kipper just hurled himself at the
ball as the giant wave crashed onto
the beach.

He grabbed, and disappeared in a
great splash of foam and water!

But over the sound of the waves,
and of the tumbling of the pebbles,
and of the bubbling of the water in
his ears, Kipper heard another sound,
a faint pop. And he felt something
collapse underneath him.

As Kipper lifted his beach ball out of the water...

...it seemed to give a sigh, and slowly it became a wrinkly thing again.

'It's sort of died!' he said to Tiger, which made them both laugh.

They tried blowing
it up again, but the
big split on one side
let the air out as fast
as they could blow.

Kipper noticed that it
smelt more plasticky than
ever, which for some
reason made him feel
suddenly sad.

'We could always buy
some more cornflakes,'
suggested Tiger.

So they hurried home to buy more
cornflakes, and ran all the way to
Kipper's house with six whole boxes,
which they emptied straight onto the floor.
But all they found were
three penguin rubbers,
two wind-up sharks,
one jumpy frog
and lots of cornflakes.

Over the next three weeks Kipper ate
nothing but cornflakes. Cornflakes for
breakfast and cornflakes for dinner too.
But there was no beach ball, and in the
end Kipper stopped looking.

Even so, each time he gets a new box of cornflakes Kipper sniffs the box before opening it, just in case there is a nice, plasticky sort of smell coming from inside.